to Sammy

Easte_____

and a very "eggstra"

special day

love love love

"Marshie"

Hop To It!

A Scholastic Easter Treasury

The Tale of Peter Rabbit
Clifford's Happy Easter
Peter Cottontail
The Best Easter Hunt Ever
Bunny Trouble
More Bunny Trouble
The Easter Ribbit

Cartwheel
·B·O·O·K·S·®

SCHOLASTIC INC.

New York Toronto London Auckland Sydney
Mexico City New Delhi Hong Kong Buenos Aires

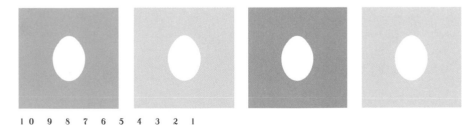

10 9 8 7 6 5 4 3 2 1   03   04   05   06   07

Printed in Singapore 46
This edition first printing, February 2003
Book design by Sarita Kusuma

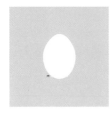

THE TALE OF PETER RABBIT

by BEATRIX POTTER

Illustrated by DAVID McPHAIL

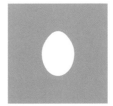

Cartwheel
B·O·O·K·S·
SCHOLASTIC INC.
New York Toronto London Auckland Sydney
Mexico City New Delhi Hong Kong Buenos Aires

ISBN 0-590-41101-2

Illustrations copyright © 1986 by David McPhail.
All rights reserved. Published by Scholastic Inc.
SCHOLASTIC, CARTWHEEL BOOKS, and associated logos are trademarks
and/or registered trademarks of Scholastic Inc.

ONCE UPON A TIME there were four little
Rabbits, and their names were —
    Flopsy,
       Mopsy,
          Cottontail,
           and Peter.

They lived with their mother in a sandbank,
underneath the root of a very big fir tree.

6

"Now, my dears," said old Mrs. Rabbit one morning, "you may go into the fields or down the lane, but don't go into Mr. McGregor's garden: your father had an accident there; he was put in a pie by Mrs. McGregor."

"Now run along, and don't get into mischief.
I am going out."

9

Then old Mrs. Rabbit took a basket and her umbrella, and went through the wood to the baker's. She bought a loaf of brown bread and five currant buns.

Flopsy, Mopsy, and Cottontail, who were good
little bunnies, went down the lane to gather
blackberries.

But Peter, who was very naughty,
ran straight away to Mr. McGregor's garden,
and squeezed under the gate!

First he ate some lettuces and
   some French beans; and
      then he ate some radishes; and
         then, feeling rather sick, he
            went to look for some parsley.

But round the end of a cucumber frame, whom should he meet but Mr. McGregor!

Mr. McGregor was on his hands and knees planting out young cabbages, but he jumped up and ran after Peter, waving a rake and calling out, "Stop thief!"

Peter was most dreadfully frightened; he rushed all over the garden, for he had forgotten the way back to the gate.

He lost one of his shoes among the cabbages, and the other shoe amongst the potatoes.

After losing them, he ran on four legs and went faster, so that I think he might have got away altogether if he had not unfortunately run into a gooseberry net, and got caught by the large buttons on his jacket. It was a blue jacket with brass buttons, quite new.

Peter gave himself up for lost, and shed big tears; but his sobs were overheard by some friendly sparrows, who flew to him in great excitement, and implored him to exert himself.

Mr. McGregor came up with a sieve, which he intended to pop upon the top of Peter; but Peter wriggled out just in time, leaving his jacket behind him, and rushed into the toolshed, and jumped into a can.

It would have been a beautiful thing to hide in, if it had not had so much water in it.

Mr. McGregor was quite sure that Peter was somewhere
in the toolshed, perhaps hidden underneath a flowerpot.
He began to turn them over carefully, looking under each.

Presently Peter sneezed — "Kertyschoo!" Mr. McGregor was after him in no time, and tried to put his foot upon Peter, who jumped out of a window, upsetting three plants. The window was too small for Mr. McGregor, and he was tired of running after Peter. He went back to his work.

Peter sat down to rest. He was out of breath and trembling with fright, and he had not the least idea which way to go. Also, he was very damp with sitting in that can.

After a time he began to wander about, going lippity — lippity — not very fast, and looking all around.

He found a door in a wall; but it was locked, and there was no room for a fat little rabbit to squeeze underneath.

An old mouse was running in and out over the stone doorstep, carrying peas and beans to her family in the wood. Peter asked her the way to the gate, but she had such a large pea in her mouth that she could not answer. She only shook her head at him.

Peter began to cry.

Then he tried to find his way straight across the garden, but he became more and more puzzled. Presently, he came to a pond where Mr. McGregor filled his water cans. A white cat was staring at some goldfish; she sat very,

24

very still, but now and then the tip of her tail twitched as if it were alive. Peter thought it best to go away without speaking to her; he had heard about cats from his cousin, little Benjamin Bunny.

He went back towards the toolshed, but suddenly, quite close to him, he heard the noise of a hoe — scr-r-ritch, scratch, scratch, scritch. Peter scuttered underneath the bushes.

But presently, as nothing happened, he came out, and climbed upon a wheelbarrow, and peeped over. The first thing he saw was Mr. McGregor hoeing onions. His back was turned towards Peter, and beyond him was the gate!

Peter got down very quietly off the wheelbarrow, and started running as fast as he could go, along a straight walk behind some black-currant bushes.

Mr. McGregor caught sight of him at the corner, but Peter did not care. He slipped underneath the gate, and was safe at last in the wood outside the garden.

Mr. McGregor hung up the little jacket and the shoes for a scarecrow to frighten the blackbirds.

Peter never stopped running or looked behind him till he got home to the big fir tree.

He was so tired that he flopped down upon the nice soft sand on the floor of the rabbit hole, and shut his eyes. His mother was busy cooking; she wondered what he had done with his clothes. It was the second little jacket and pair of shoes that Peter had lost in a fortnight!

I am sorry to say that Peter was not very well during the evening.

His mother put him to bed, and made some camomile tea; and she gave a dose of it to Peter!

"One tablespoonful to be taken at bedtime."

But Flopsy, Mopsy, and Cottontail had bread and milk and blackberries for supper.

THE END.

CLIFFORD'S HAPPY EASTER

by NORMAN BRIDWELL

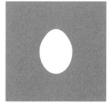

Cartwheel
B·O·O·K·S ®
SCHOLASTIC INC.
New York Toronto London Auckland Sydney
Mexico City New Delhi Hong Kong Buenos Aires

For Lauren Nicole Delker

ISBN 0-590-47782-X

Hi! I'm Emily Elizabeth, and I love spring.
So does my dog Clifford.

The best part of springtime is Easter.

Last spring Mom and Dad brought us
a lot of eggs to color for the big Easter egg hunt.

On the day before Easter, I dyed the eggs.
Clifford wanted to help.
Poor Clifford. He wasn't very good at painting eggs.

So Clifford helped by watching me decorate the eggs.
He's a good watcher.

When I went to bed that night,
I fell asleep dreaming about Easter eggs.

It was a beautiful dream. Clifford was stirring
a giant tub of dye while I tossed in the eggs.

But then Clifford lost his balance!
He tumbled into the tub of dye.

Something surprising began to happen....

Suddenly Clifford was bright green!

It was just like St. Patrick's Day.

Then he turned sunshine-yellow!
This was becoming a very strange dream.

I grabbed a brush and began to dab on purple polka dots.
Clifford looked good in polka dots, but —

— they didn't last long.
The purple dots turned into squares,
and Clifford looked like . . .

...a giant checkerboard!

I didn't like that. I threw on some more dye.

Clifford started to change colors again.

Now he was red, white, and blue!

I always used to wonder if I dreamed in color.
Now I know.

This was too much.

I tried to scrub the dye off Clifford. I was getting frantic...

...then I woke up.
It was Easter morning, and the sun was shining.

I ran out to see Clifford.

Thank goodness he looked just the same as always.

Good old Clifford.

We joined my friends and set off on the Easter egg hunt.

We looked high.

We looked low.

Clifford looked in places I would not have thought of.

No hiding place was missed.

Sometimes Clifford went a little too far.

His hard work helped.
We ended up with heaps of eggs...

...which we shared with our friends.
After all, friends are what make Easter a happy day.

PETER COTTONTAIL

by AMANDA STEPHENS

Illustrated by CHRISTOPHER SANTORO

Cartwheel
B·O·O·K·S ®

SCHOLASTIC INC.

New York Toronto London Auckland Sydney
Mexico City New Delhi Hong Kong Buenos Aires

To Jaime
— **C.S.**

ISBN 0-590-47761-7

Easter was always the best day of the year in Green Valley. That was the day Peter Cottontail came to town. "Higglety pigglety, here I am!" Peter would always say.

Every year, Peter brought Easter baskets filled with bright, beautifully colored eggs and sweet, yummy candies. There was a basket for each of the children.

"Higglety pigglety, happy Easter!" Peter would shout as he hopped from house to house.

On Easter morning the mommies would parade in their new Easter bonnets. The children would munch on their Easter candy.

In Green Valley, every Easter was exactly the same as the one before.

Until one year, on the day before Easter...

Wily Wolf decided there would be no more Easter fun in Green Valley.

"Those bunnies make such a big deal out of Easter," Wily grumbled to himself. "They sing, and they dance, and they feast — and they never invite me! Well, I'll show them. Peter Cottontail won't be giving out any Easter eggs this year!"

Then Wily hid behind a tree and waited for Peter to come hopping by.

It wasn't long before Peter Cottontail appeared at the top of the hill.

As soon as Wily spotted the happy rabbit, he let out a loud, ferocious *ROAR!* That *ROAR* sure scared Peter! He dropped all of his eggs.

Quick as a wink, Wily scooped up the eggs and ran into the forest. On his way, he hid each and every egg. Wily wanted to make sure no one would find them.

The next morning, when the children awoke, there were no colored eggs anywhere. There were no jelly beans. There wasn't a chocolate bunny to be found.

"Oh, dear," cried the littlest bunny. "Peter Cottontail has forgotten all about Easter."

Of course, Peter Cottontail had not forgotten about Easter at all. He was out searching for his missing Easter eggs.

"This is higglety pigglety horrible!" Peter said sadly to himself as he hopped along.

Just then, Peter heard somebody singing in a rough, gruff voice.

"I've got the eggs, so folks won't be
Full of laughs and cheer
Without the sweets and yummy treats
There will be no Easter this year."

"So that's it," Peter said to himself. "Wily doesn't have the Easter spirit. Well, I can fix that, or *my* name isn't Peter Cottontail. Which it higglety pigglety most certainly is!"

Peter hopped back to Green Valley and told everyone what he had discovered.

"Wily Wolf has stolen all of our eggs," Peter said.
"But that does not stop us from having an Easter party.
We can still sing songs and dance and feast on deli-
cious foods."

As the other bunnies hopped off to start the party,
the littlest bunny said, "I knew Peter Cottontail could
never forget about Easter!"

Peter did not go with the other rabbits. Instead, he hurried off in search of Wily Wolf. That was a very brave thing to do — especially since wolves are not usually very nice to rabbits!

When Peter arrived at Wily's house he called, "Wily Wolf, come out here!"

Wily came out with a big smile on his face. "What are you doing here?" he asked Peter. "I thought you would be off having a big Easter party. But I see you have no Easter eggs. I guess that means Easter is cancelled."

"Not at all, Wily," Peter said sweetly. "But it would be a nicer Easter for everyone if you would just give me back the eggs you stole."

"There are no eggs here." Wily grinned. "See for yourself."

Peter looked around him. All he saw was an empty basket. Peter couldn't understand how that could be.

Just then the littlest bunny came hopping up behind Peter. "Hey, Peter! Look what I found!" In his paw was a beautiful Easter egg.

"Me, too! I found one, too!" shouted another little bunny. "It was hidden under that rock over there."

"So that's what you did with the eggs," Peter said to Wily. "Well, since you hid the eggs, you can help us find them. Come on everyone. Let's hunt for Easter eggs!"

So Wily joined the Easter egg hunt. And he had a very good time. "I like Easter," Wily smiled. "And I love Easter egg hunts! This is the best Easter I ever had!"

And all the animals in Green Valley agreed. In fact, Peter Cottontail decided to hold an Easter egg hunt every single year!

"Higglety pigglety, HOORAY!" everyone cheered.

There are 76 Easter eggs on the pages of this story.
Can you find them all?

THE BEST
EASTER HUNT
EVER

by JOHN SPEIRS

Cartwheel BOOKS ®

SCHOLASTIC INC.

New York Toronto London Auckland Sydney
Mexico City New Delhi Hong Kong Buenos Aires

To Siggy, Tilly, Rolly, Alexandra, and John

ISBN 0-590-95624-8

How to Use This Book

These children are going on an Easter hunt.
You can, too. Use the rebuses.
Look for the hidden Easter treats in the colorful pictures.
On a sheet of paper, keep track of how many Easter treats
each child finds — Roy, Sara, Tina, Alexis, John, and you.
Who finds the most treats?

The answers to the puzzles are at the end of the story.

The excited children wake up early to begin the best Easter hunt ever.

Sara finds

Roy finds

Tina finds

John finds

Alexis finds

But they couldn't find

Can you?

They race to the garden.

Sara finds

Roy finds

Tina finds

John finds

Alexis finds

But they couldn't find

Can you?

They run along the country lanes.

Sara finds

Roy finds

Tina finds

John finds

Alexis finds

But they couldn't find

Can you?

Next they walk through the village.

Sara finds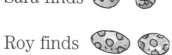

Roy finds

Tina finds

John finds

Alexis finds

But they couldn't find

Can you?

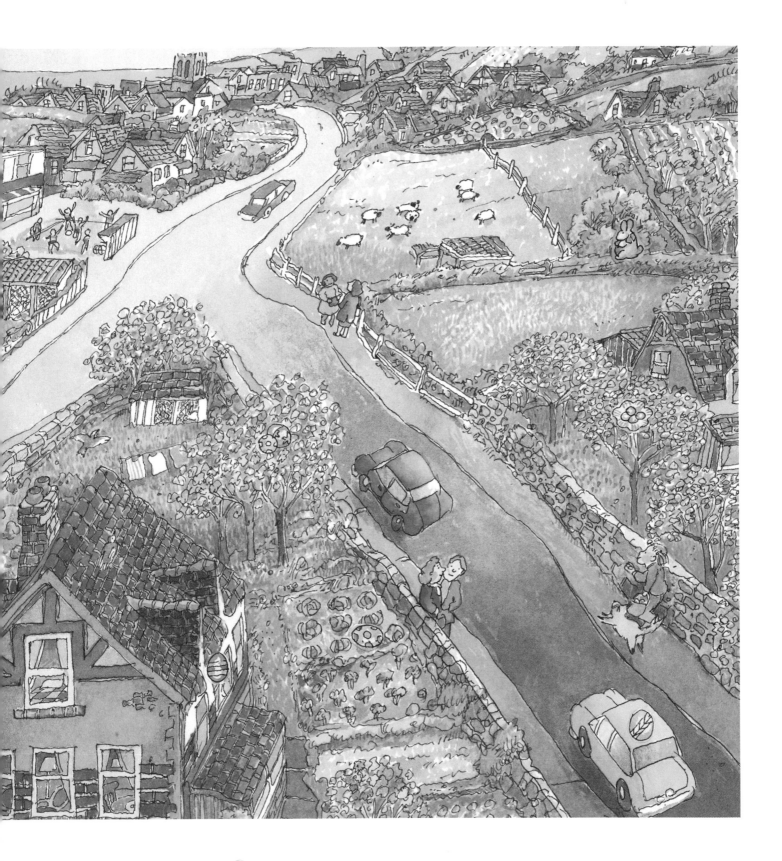

The school yard is a great place to look for treats.

Sara finds

Roy finds

Tina finds

John finds

Alexis finds

But they couldn't find

Can you?

The children look along the
riverbank and across the
bridge that leads to town.

Sara finds

Roy finds

Tina finds

John finds

Alexis finds

But they couldn't find

Can you?

They hurry through the busy streets.

Sara finds

Roy finds

Tina finds

John finds

Alexis finds

But they couldn't find

Can you?

Searching far and wide,

Sara finds

Roy finds

Tina finds

John finds

Alexis finds

But they couldn't find

Can you?

They go on to the fair
where lots of Easter treats
are waiting.

Sara finds

Roy finds

Tina finds

John finds

Alexis finds

But they couldn't find

Can you?

What fun to look along the boardwalk!

Sara finds

Roy finds

Tina finds

John finds

Alexis finds

But they couldn't find

Can you?

Home again—
just in time for an Easter party!

Sara finds

Roy finds

Tina finds

John finds

Alexis finds

But they couldn't find

Can you?

Answers

The excited children wake up early to begin the best Easter hunt ever.

Sara finds

Roy finds

Tina finds

John finds

Alexis finds

But they couldn't find

Can you?

They race to the garden.

Sara finds

Roy finds

Tina finds

John finds

Alexis finds

But they couldn't find

Can you?

Answers

They run along the country lanes.

Sara finds

Roy finds

Tina finds

John finds

Alexis finds

But they couldn't find

Can you?

Next they walk through the village.

Sara finds

Roy finds

Tina finds

John finds

Alexis finds

But they couldn't find

Can you?

Answers

The school yard is a great place to look for treats.

Sara finds

Roy finds

Tina finds

John finds

Alexis finds

But they couldn't find

Can you?

The children look along the riverbank and across the bridge that leads to town.

Sara finds

Roy finds

Tina finds

John finds

Alexis finds

But they couldn't find

Can you?

Answers

They hurry through the busy streets.

Sara finds

Roy finds

Tina finds

John finds

Alexis finds

But they couldn't find

Can you?

Searching far and wide,

Sara finds

Roy finds

Tina finds

John finds

Alexis finds

But they couldn't find

Can you?

Answers

They go on to the fair where lots of Easter treats are waiting.

Sara finds

Roy finds

Tina finds

John finds

Alexis finds

But they couldn't find

Can you?

What fun to look along the boardwalk!

Sara finds

Roy finds

Tina finds

John finds

Alexis finds

But they couldn't find

Can you?

Answers

Home again—
just in time for an Easter party!

Sara finds

Roy finds

Tina finds

John finds

Alexis finds

But they couldn't find

Can you?

Sara found 24 Easter treats.

Roy found 25 Easter treats.

Tina found 21 Easter treats.

John found 23 Easter treats.

Alexis found 19 Easter treats.

Did you find 14 Easter treats?

Roy is the winner!

BUNNY TROUBLE

by HANS WILHELM

Cartwheel
·B·O·O·K·S·®

SCHOLASTIC INC.

New York Toronto London Auckland Sydney
Mexico City New Delhi Hong Kong Buenos Aires

ISBN 0-590-45042-5

Once there was a rabbit colony that was different from any other. The rabbits here were in charge of decorating all the Easter eggs for the Easter Bunny to deliver.

Everyone worked year 'round getting ready.

Everyone except Ralph. He cared for only one thing in the world—soccer.

It worried his mother and father.

It worried the other rabbits in the colony.

It worried his teachers in the school where all the young rabbits went to learn egg decorating. Where was Ralph while everyone else was hard at work in the classroom? He was outside working on his fancy footwork.

It worried his sister Liza—especially when he ruined her birthday party.

Liza loved Ralph more than anyone else in the world. But she knew that one day he would get into trouble. He just didn't fit in.

Each year as Easter approached, everyone got busier and busier. The chickens laid more eggs. The painters, the jelly bean makers, and the basket stuffers all worked overtime.

Ralph had to work, too. But he had a hard time keeping his mind on his job.

Instead, he was thinking about place kicks, and he tried just one. Oooops! Over went a full basket of eggs.

The exhausted chickens groaned. The rabbits shouted at Ralph. "Go play soccer on the other side of the trees so we can finish our work in peace," they said.

Ralph was glad to go. He went off to play by himself on the other side of the forest.

That night, he did not come home.

His mother wept and wrung her hands. "Where could he be?" she wondered. "And with Easter just two days away."

Morning came. Still Ralph had not come home. Liza slipped out to search for him.

She found him not far away — locked up in a cage.

A farmer had caught him while he was practicing his dribble in the cauliflower field.

"The coach always told us to look where we were going, not at our feet," Ralph joked sorrowfully.

"Don't worry," Liza told him. "I'll go and get help."

She ran back, past the busy rabbits, calling,
"Mama, mama, we must save Ralph. The farmer
has caught him and is going to make him into
Easter dinner!"

"Oh, I knew that bunny would get into
trouble someday," wept mama as she
followed Liza to Ralph's cage.

It had thick bars and a heavy padlock.

"We'll never get him out of there," moaned their mother when she saw Ralph inside.

"Of course we will," said Liza firmly. "I think I can get the lock open."

Liza worked for
hours. But the lock
refused to be picked.
The bars wouldn't bend.
The door couldn't be
pried off.

"If I ever get free," whispered Ralph, "I promise I will never play soccer again."

"No, Ralph," said Liza, "you want to be a soccer player. And you will be, too. But you also have to help with the eggs."

"And not be such a nuisance," added mama.

Ralph knew they were right. He promised to do what they said.

Hours passed. Suddenly Liza cried, "I've got an idea that will do the trick! But we have to hurry."

Liza and mama ran all the way home. In no time, Liza was back carrying a small bundle under her arms. She squeezed it carefully through the bars of Ralph's cage. Then she whispered the plan.

The next morning there was a
great commotion around the cage.

Inside it, next to Ralph, was a basket of the most beautiful Easter eggs anyone had ever seen. Some were polka-dotted, some were dyed deep purple, and some were painted with rainbows.

The farmer's children gathered around. "He must be the Easter Bunny," they exclaimed with wonder. "How else could he have gotten those eggs? We must let him go or there won't be any Easter for us."

So the farmer opened the cage door.

Ralph ran home as fast as he could.

But he didn't forget Liza's words. He did try harder with his painting.

Ralph even became known for one special design, which he did far better than anyone else, and almost as well as kicking, passing, and scoring.

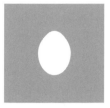

More
Bunny Trouble

by Hans Wilhelm

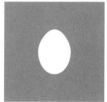

Cartwheel
·B·O·O·K·S·®
SCHOLASTIC INC.
New York Toronto London Auckland Sydney
Mexico City New Delhi Hong Kong Buenos Aires

On the day before Easter, Ralph was out kicking his soccer ball—just what he liked to do most.

Then his mother told him to watch his little sister Emily—just what he didn't like to do most.

He couldn't understand why his mother and father made such a fuss about Emily. She cried a lot and was always wet.

Ralph thought Emily must be the noisiest, messiest baby in the whole world.

Ralph's mother gave him some Easter eggs to decorate and a blanket to sit on.

"Be sure that your sister does not crawl into the tall grass," she told Ralph.

Ralph was trying to concentrate on his painting when Emily reached over to touch the eggs.

"Stop that!" Ralph said, and he poked her with his paw. Not too hard, but not too gently, either—just enough to make Emily cry.

Mama came running. "What's the matter with Emily?" she asked Ralph.

"I don't know," Ralph said, pretending to be busy painting an egg.

But Ralph's mother had a good idea of what had happened. "Ralph, I have told you over and over again—paws are not made for hitting."

Ralph bowed his head. "Yes, mama," he said.

But as soon as their mother was back inside, Ralph poked his little sister again.

Emily cried and cried. But this time her mother did not come. Instead two butterflies flew by and fluttered around Emily's head.

She quickly forgot about the hurt and started after the pretty blue creatures.

Emily crawled off the
blanket and headed straight for
the tall green grass.

It was a whole new world
for Emily, filled with animals
and flowers she had never seen
before.

Everything was so pretty and
smelled so good. Emily looked
around, and then she went on
crawling. On and on....

Suddenly Ralph looked up and saw that his sister was gone!

"Oh, no!" he cried. "I was supposed to be watching her. Where did she go? How did she get away so fast?"

"EMILY!" he called as loudly as he could. "E-M-I-L-Y!" But there was no answer.

Ralph looked
everywhere. He listened,
trying to hear his sister's
cry. Nothing.

"Oh, dear! She must have
gone into the tall grass!
Anything could happen in
there. A fox could get her,
or an eagle, or a snake...I
have to find her!"

But the grass was so tall Ralph could not see anything.

He ran to his mother and
told her the whole story.

Ralph's mother did not lose
any time. She called the
neighbors together and asked
them to help her find the baby.

All the rabbits were busy
getting eggs ready for Easter.
But this was more important.
They stopped their work and
ran out into the tall grass.

Each rabbit set off in a different direction. The field was so large and there were so few rabbits—how could they possibly search every spot? Besides, in the thick grass, they could easily pass right by the baby without even seeing her.

"Emily! Emily!" they cried.

Still no answer.

Where was Emily? Could she hear them?

Someone did hear the rabbits calling. It was a fox!
He knew immediately what had happened.

He licked his chops. "With a little bit of luck, I'll have myself a delicious baby rabbit for supper!" he said.

And with that, the fox joined the search for little Emily.

Emily's mother was getting frantic. "It's late," she cried. "We have to find Emily before the sun goes down."

"We need more help," said one of the neighbors. "The grass is so thick and tall and there are so few of us."

Then Ralph spoke up. "I know what we can do! Listen, everybody. I think I have the answer."

The rabbits stopped their search and gathered around Ralph.

"Here is my idea," Ralph said. "We will all hold paws together and walk in a long line across the field. That way we can cover every inch. We can't miss her."

All the rabbits thought this was a good idea. They joined paws and combed through the tall grass.

And that's how they found
little Emily, fast asleep, dreaming
of butterflies.

There were cheers as Ralph's mother took Emily into her arms again.

Everyone was overjoyed. Even Ralph shed a tear or two.

With the baby home safe at last, the rabbits could finish the Easter eggs in time.

It would be a happy Easter for all—except, of course, for the fox!

From then on, Ralph watched his favorite sister very carefully.

The two of them could often be seen walking along, holding paws together.

THE EASTER RIBBIT

by BERNICE CHARDIET

Illustrated by CHARLES MICUCCI

Cartwheel
·B·O·O·K·S·®

SCHOLASTIC INC.

New York Toronto London Auckland Sydney
Mexico City New Delhi Hong Kong Buenos Aires

To Jane, Margaret, and Cole Chardiet,
with all my love
— B.C.

To Lindsey, Sophia, and Marcus
— C.M.

ISBN 0-590-10072-6

Text copyright © 1998 by Chardiet Unlimited, Inc.
Illustrations copyright © 1998 by Charles Micucci.
All rights reserved. Published by Scholastic Inc.
SCHOLASTIC, CARTWHEEL BOOKS, and associated logos are trademarks
and/or registered trademarks of Scholastic Inc.

Easter was coming. The bunnies were very busy making pretty Easter baskets, carrying jelly beans, and painting eggs.

Froggie watched them from the pond.
Sometimes he wished he were a rabbit.
They seemed to be having so much fun.

Hmmm! Maybe he could convince Turtle to let him paint her eggs before they hatched.

Froggie quickly ran to the beach. Turtle was there covering her eggs with sand.

"Ribbit! Ribbit!" Froggie called to Turtle. "It's almost Easter! May I paint your eggs?"

"Keep quiet!" Turtle warned. "Can't you see I'm trying to hide them? If you were to paint them, every bird in the forest would see my eggs and eat them before the babies could hatch and crawl to the water. Go back to your log and stop bothering me!"

Froggie walked sadly to his favorite hollow log near the rabbit tree and crawled inside. After a long time of feeling sorry for himself, he fell asleep and had a dream.

In the dream he was an Easter Ribbit—not quite a rabbit but not a frog either. He was rushing through the high grass to deliver Easter baskets to all the children. The baskets were full of things that Froggie loved: jelly beans, lollipops, flies, tiny fish eggs, seaweed bars, and delicious mosquitoes, too.

Suddenly a terrible noise woke Froggie.
He opened his eyes and peeked out of the log.

The Chief Easter Bunny had just landed in a helicopter.
He was carrying armfuls of lists of all the children who
needed Easter presents. Mrs. Rabbit and all of her
assistants came running out to greet him.

"You are doing a wonderful job!" said the Chief. "But we need more helpers! Can you handle an extra load of deliveries?"

"Oh, dear," said Mrs. Rabbit. "We don't have enough bunnies to deliver the baskets! Flossie and Fernie caught colds last night and I'm afraid they are running fevers. And Hubert and Henry hurt their feet squeezing under a fence. They can't run until next week. What will we do?"

"Advertise!" said the Chief Easter Bunny.

"Call Mrs. Duck's Employment Agency. She can fly over the woods and drop ads for the position *tonight*! Mrs. Duck's a quack but she may be able to help us."

"All right," said Mrs. Rabbit. "We'll do our best!"

Mrs. Duck was sound asleep when Mrs. Rabbit called, but she woke up and wrote the ad anyway. Unfortunately, Mrs. Duck was very nearsighted and didn't see her spelling mistake. Instead of writing an ad for an Easter Rabbit, she had written an ad for an Easter *Ribbit*.

HELP
WANTED
—
EASTER
RIBBIT

HELP
WANTED
—
EASTER
RIBBIT

HELP
WANTED
—
EASTER
RIBBIT

HE
WAN
EASTER
RIBBIT

One of the ads landed on Froggie's log. Froggie saw it as soon as he woke up the next morning. "An Easter Ribbit?" said Froggie. "That's me!" It was his dream come true! Quickly, he wrote down Mrs. Duck's address and ran to the employment office.

Although she couldn't see well, Mrs. Duck suspected that she was looking at a frog. Nevertheless, Froggie was the only client who had come into her office for a very long time, and there wasn't a rabbit in sight.

Mrs. Duck ran to her storage room and cut out a big pair of paper bunny ears. She tied them on Froggie's head. Then Mrs. Duck pasted a big cotton ball on Froggie to make a rabbit's tail.

Froggie was divinely happy. He ran to Mrs. Rabbit's tree right away.

Mrs. Rabbit and all her assistants were working feverishly to color new eggs and fill new baskets. Glancing quickly at Froggie's big, floppy ears, Mrs. Rabbit didn't notice that he was an Easter Ribbit—and not an Easter Rabbit. She pointed to a tall tower of Easter baskets outside the back door and told Froggie to start his deliveries.

Froggie looked up at the baskets. "Ribbit!" he gasped. "I'll never be able to deliver all of these by Easter!"

There was only one thing to do. Quickly, he hopped down to the pond. Ribbiting as loudly as he could, Froggie called for all of his friends and relatives to come and help him. Soon a crowd of frogs of all shapes and sizes leapfrogged to pick up the baskets stacked behind Mrs. Rabbit's tree.

And if you had been anywhere near Froggie's log at the crack of dawn on Easter morning, you would have seen them marching through the meadow to deliver the Easter baskets to the children. And at the head of the parade was Froggie, ribbiting a happy song.

FROGGIE'S

I'm a froggie in a hurry,

And I've really got to scurry

Before the sun comes up.

While all the kids are sleeping,

I'll be hopping, sprinting, leaping.

I'm as happy as a pup.

I can't be a rabbit,

SONG

So I'll be an Easter Ribbit.

It's true I'm green, but if I'm seen,

I really can ad-lib it.

I'll leave some Easter baskets,

And everyone will cheer.

A tisket, a tasket,

The Ribbit has been here!

And from that day to this, if you listen carefully you will always hear the little frogs called "peepers" singing in the woods in early spring. They are telling the story of Froggie the Easter Ribbit and how he became a hero to little frogs everywhere.

FROGGIE'S SONG